Skellig Testament

An historic novella.

David Rory O'Neill

davidrory-publishing
Newport, Tipperary, Ireland

David Rory O'Neill. davidrory-publishing
Newport, Tipperary, Ireland.
www.davidrory.net

Publisher's Note: This is a work of fiction. Names, characters, places, and incidents are a product of the author's imagination. Locales and public names are sometimes used for atmospheric purposes. Any resemblance to actual people, living or dead, or to businesses, companies, events, institutions, or locales is completely coincidental.

Ordering Information: Quantity sales. Special discounts are available on quantity purchases by corporations, associations, and others.

For details, contact: www. davidrory.com

Skellig Testament/ David Rory O'Neill. 4th ed. 2118
ISBN- ISBN-13: 978-1497439344
ISBN-10: 1497439345

Dedications:
My thanks go to Miriam Drori for editorial help and
encouragement.
For Brigitte who showed me what love can be.
For Ria who is loved and is my one true legacy and who now has
given me a grandson – Art Leonis Parker Elliott.

Cover Design by Samantha at Ebookcoversgalore.com
Artwork and illustrations by the author.
Book Layout ©2013 BookDesignTemplates.com

David Rory O'Neill. Ireland. 2018.

UK English is used in this work.

*If you enjoyed this novel please leave a review on your
suppliers' site or on Goodreads – reviews are the lifeblood
of the modern author. Thank you.*

ABOUT THE AUTHOR
David Rory O'Neill

Born and raised in Belfast until troubles and tribal violence drove him away, David grew to be a non-conformist and independent soul clinging to his counter-culture ideals. He found peace and his true calling as a storyteller in the literary Irish tradition. He now lives in a lovely restored old art and book-filled house in the lee of the Silvermine Mountains, Tipperary, Ireland. He shares his life there with beloved Brigitte. David Rory O'Neill has written twenty novels and more are bubbling and brewing.

http://www.davidroy.com

Contents:

Introduction:

This is entirely a work of imaginative fiction. Historically accurate were possible but fiction nevertheless.

This story is an attempt to understand what drove men to build a monastery on a near vertical pillar of rock off the coast of Ireland.

The author has sought to use imagination to bring to life the men who were driven to seek this kind of complete isolation. More than hermits, more than any other monks, they choose a life filled with hardship, back braking labour and danger. The results of their efforts that remain are among the best-preserved buildings from the period. The Skellig monastery is a world heritage site and rightly so. It is unique and thrilling place to visit.

Even if you don't feel up to the massive climb and a sea tossed journey by boat, you can still get a feel for the place in the visitor centre at Valencia.

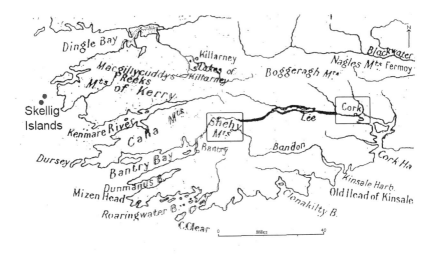

Sothern Ireland, the province of Munster showing the Skellig Islands

CHAPTER ONE

an Corcach Mó.

THE GREAT MARSH, NOW CALLED: CORK.

The Climate in Ireland changed in a dramatic way beginning around 1200. The Atlantic currents that had bathed the island in warmth changed course slightly, resulting in a drop in temperature, an increase in the severity of winter storms and increased rainfall. This made the tiny island of Skellig off the southwest tip of county Kerry uninhabitable. The twelve monks who still lived there were forced to move to the abbey at Ballinskelligs on the mainland.

The history of the founding of the Skellig monastery and hermitage is lost to us and until recently, no written record existed.

The modern Saint Fin Barre's Cathedral. Cork.

A few years ago an ancient book was unearthed in the records of Saint Fin Barre's Cathedral in Cork City. This document, hand written in Latin, was in poor condition and not thought to be of any great significance. The title pages were missing and therefore the subject was not thought important, one of many transcripts of ancient Latin and Creek manuscripts found in Irish monastic scriptorium. The book, showed none of the usual illuminations and decoration to be found on the more noteworthy ancient works. The Book of Kells, on display in Trinity College Dublin, perhaps being the most well known example.

The book was put aside for future translation among many others stored in the deep cellars beneath the Cathedral. It might have remained there had it not been for the now normal torrential rainfall and flooding modern Cork is prone to.

The author happened to be at a musical recital in the Cathedral that was interrupted by a sudden and potentially catastrophic breech of the cellar walls that threatened to inundate the place. Volunteers were called for to help remove the cases and bundles stored there. Seventy or so people formed a human chain to bring musty packages up the stairs past the sunken organ into the body of the church, safe from the fast rising waters.

When all was done and we stood around dripping, excited and drinking tea provided by the vergers' wife, I happened to have an old cloth wrapped book close to hand. I asked if I might examine it and was given permission by the Deacon. I sat at a pew and carefully unwrapped the book. It was written on parchment, sheep's skin, and was plain and not illuminated. The binding was missing, as were the first few pages. The Latin was an ancient form not familiar to me but my eye was arrested by two words on the first intact page: Sceilig Mhór.

I knew this to be Irish not Latin and I also knew the meaning: Skellig Island. I was unreasonably excited by this and spent the next few hours pouring over the script trying to translate what I could. It soon became evident that this was a first hand account of life in the ancient hermitage and monastery. I spoke to the Dean and he became as excited as I, when I explained the significance. By then I'd found several references to Fionnbharr. This being the Irish name for the founder of the church we now sat in and indeed the city of Cork. We arranged for the script to be removed to a Latin specialist at University College Cork for translation. I was promised special access to the results as the work progressed.

This then is the result of that work. A personal testament written in the early monastic settlement started by Fin Barre overlooking the great swamp and marsh that gave its name to Cork. Corcach. The scribe was Brother Edan, (Aidan) then an old man living out his last days in the monastery that had trained him as a youth and that now gave him refuge in his old age.

The author has translated the ancient language idioms to modern English in order to make this fascinating account more accessible to the reader. Literary licence is used where gaps existed, in order to aid the flow of the story through time. Modern names are also used for places and people to save the reader the chore of footnotes. No liberties have been taken with facts. The story begins in the then new monastic settlement of Fin Barre on a small cliff overlooking the marsh where the river Lee becomes tidal at the mouth of the great harbour, later to be called Cork. The year is 676.

This then is Brother Edan's testament:

This being the personal and true testament of Brother Edan written in the year of our lord 676 at the Abby of *Fionnbhar*. In the region of *Corcach*.

I was born into this world in the year 608 or 609. There is some uncertainty about this for my father, Oran had not learning and knew not what the number of the years might be. He was settled on a hill over the lake of Gur and there farmed oat and barley and cabbage. He had sheep twenty, goats ten and cattle six. There where foul and ducks and fish from the lake so we fed well in the early years of my childhood. There were two brothers before me and two more after and three girls. Three infants did not live past their first year.

My mother, Etromma was said to be of royal blood but there was little way to know this but for her carriage and ways which were not like the other women of the settlement. She had reading and taught her children the words of the scripture she had as treasure from her family.

This is how I first learned the holy language of Latin. I was put to reading at an early age and have no memory when this was. As a small boy I was asked to read the scripture aloud everyday before the meal of the evening. After, mother would say the blessings and we would then eat our soup or stew.

Father brewed ale from barley and I remember when I first drank too much and was sick before bedtime. I might have been eight years then. I swore I would not drink it again but there was little else but milk that I did not care for and still cannot stomach with out biliousness.

1

One summer when I might have reached eleven years, we had a visit from a travelling monk whose name I cannot now in memory find. He stayed in our house and read the scriptures to us, changing the words to the Irish for those of my brothers and sisters who had not the Latin. The holy man had come from the Abby of *Fionnbhar* in the mountains at the source of the river of the Lee at Loch Irce.

He spoke to me of the life of the monks of his order and I became sure then I wanted to be as he was and take the holy vows. He said I must wait until my fifteenth year before I could become a postulant.

My family was by then struggling to feed us all and father said it would be wise if I left to find a home, feeding and shelter in the Abby. I must confess here, I did not wait for my fifteen years. But left home two years later. I might have been thirteen or fourteen when I set out to walk to the Abby of *Fionnbhar.* The holy man had left me a parchment with lines showing my route and words of introduction to the Abbott.

The tracks I followed were not well trodden at first and my progress was slow. I stopped to gather oak-apples in the forests. We called these 'inky-balls' and they are boiled up to make ink for writing. The travelling holy man had told me they would welcome all I could bring at the abbey.

I reached a settlement on a mighty black river. There was a forde there and I got fair chilled crossing. On the far bank a family gave me shelter and let me sit by their turf fire to dry and warm. They gave me a gruel of groats with a little mutton. In truth the mutton was rancid and still had wool on it. I struggled to eat it down but didn't want to cause hurt by refusing their kindness. I slept with their beasts in the bier since their little house had sixteen sleeping in. I did not mind the company of the cow, moke *(donkey)* and sheep. I do not like the smell of tallow lamps and sleep outside in the freshness of the air at home when I can.

As I travelled on, I found the track busier with drovers walking cattle, goat and sheep. I learned that they were walking to a big new settlement in the marsh on the Lee. They said many sea boats come there to trade from far and even from a land across the mighty sea. One I walked with told me that Abbott Fin Barre had made a monastery on the edge of the marsh and this is why the people came and built a village on an island before the holy place. So now I knew I didn't need to go to the mountains at Loch Irce.

Two days did we walk until we stood on the hill to the north of the marsh. On the far bank of the river and marsh, which had many islands and channels, I saw the Abby. There was a mighty tower that stood above the walls of wood. It was a surprise to my eyes. I'd never seen or imagined a place could rise so far. Below the little white cliff, a town spread on to a big island. A wood wall encompassed it with gates at the south and north side. The only way to approach from the north hills were we stood, was by boat of which there were many traversing the river from our side. They went through the gates and into the channel in the middle of the settlement.

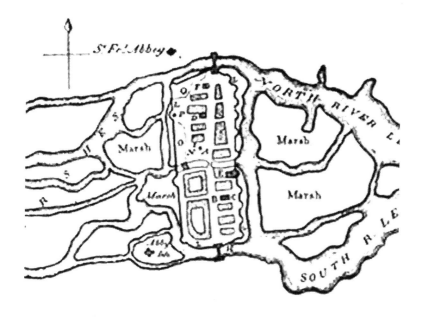

Cork as it was around the year 1100.

I have never seen so many people gathered before, and in truth I found the sight frighted me. There was much noise and shouting as we waited to be ferried across. The drovers all yelled and screamed to encourage their beasts, most as frighted as me, on to the boats. A fee of coin was charged to be ferried over. My father had given me a purse with silver coin and one gold. The smallest silver was given and three copper were got back. I was glad to travel on a small curragh and not the big ones that had the beasts upon them. One cow jumped off and made a great bellowing as it swam near the boat. The boatmen beat it with their oars to stop it trying to regain the curragh. It near upturned the boat in it's striving.

When ashore I was greeted by a great stink from the streams and puddles of excrement in the way. There was tumult and more people than I'd ever seen before. Their dwellings and trading places were pressed close down the whole length of the main. As I walked, they shouted at me to buy their goods but their words were not easy for me to know. They sounded their speech in ways strange to my ears.

It took me a passing long time to make my way the length of the path in the middle of the settlement such was the crush of people and beasts. I noted some of the beasts that had made the crossing where being butchered as soon as they came ashore. It made a frightening noise and sight. I have seen butchery before but not like this, not surrounded by people. Many ragged women and children gathered all around the slaughter house and the animal was cut and passed to them for coin before it was stopped bleeding. The inners and organs were first and most wanted. I decided these were much in demand for their price being low, only a few copper coin. The women had baskets to carry off the meats, still dripping blood.

When I passed through the gate at the south of the settlement I saw the abbey rising before me on a small hill. The path to the gate rose on steps cut in the stone of the cliff. I found my way barred by a large wooden gate. A yellow metal shape hung near with a stick to strike it, or so it seemed to me. I later learned this was a bell but I'd never seen or heard one before I struck it on that day. The bell made a loud but pleasant noise so I struck it thrice. The gate was opened by a holy man in a brown robe who was not best pleased with me for sounding the bell so much.

I made my sorries and showed him the parchment I carried introducing me. He led me in to the biggest building that was made of stones and wood and that had a wood roof of split woods like plates. It was the biggest building I'd ever seen and I was a little afraid as I stepped in. It was dark like evening with lamps about the walls and on tables. Monks worked all around at various labours but the one nearest me crouched over a parchment writing the Latin words with a large goose quill. I remembered my bag of inky-balls and got them from my sack. I asked the monk who was writing if I should give them to him. He spoke without lifting his head saying: "Give them to brother Edan, the Cellarer."

I was shocked to hear another with my name. I did not know that the Cellarer was the brother charged with provisioning of the monastery.

My name was called and I was lead to a small room at the back of the abbey. There sat a man with yellow gold hair and a kind face. "I am Find Barre, Abbot here. Your letter tells me you wish to be postulate here. Sit boy and tell me why you want to join our order."

I was stunned by this simple question for I'd never asked myself why. It simply seemed the thing I must do. I said this and the Abbott laughed and said, "As good an answer as any I've heard.

I suddenly knew why this holy man and was called *Fionnbhar* for those words mean 'fair hair' or 'fair head.'

He told me what life as monk would mean and asked me many times if I knew what this would mean for me and if I was sure it was what I wanted. His words made me question what I was doing for the first time. I grew less frighted as each moment past so when I had been with the

Abbot for a long time I was sure that this was the life I wanted.

The idea of being alone, being given time to think and pray and consider the scriptures and live with others that were the same, all these things I was sure I wanted. And learning, above all learning was a great hunger in me. Learning the skills and trades the Abbot told me of. He said I did not need to decided until after my final vows and that would be years ahead. He then send me to the monk he called the Barber Surgeon to have my first tonsure. The hair cut from the top of my head and shaved in a circle, this is the mark of the monk and I was proud and excited as I sat on the stool while the old man cut and shaved my head. I had a few cuts that bled a little but I did not mind. I saw myself in a glass after and was pleased.

I was then sent to the Cellarer to be given a robe and sandals and a small scripture for my studies. My old clothes where taken and burnt and all I'd brought with me was taken. Even my coin. I was fierce about that until I was told a monk needed no coin. Only the willingness to work hard and study. All my needs would be provided by God and the order I was now to join.

CHAPTER TWO

Postulate.

ruth be told now, I have little memory of those early days of study and work as a postulate and novice. It seemed time past so quickly and each day became as the next and the one that past. Each day divided into Matins, Lauds, Prime, Terce, Sext, Nones, Vespers and Compine. These are the daily devotions when work stopped and we assembled for praying and chanting and reading the scriptures and the words of the Abbot. The day began before the light and ended early. Each day the same as the last but for the holy day when service and devotions where many.

I come now to a difficult thing I am not sure I should reveal. Many novices I saw suffered silently and went to their graves not confessed of this thing. Many people believe that holy orders are places without sin and will be unkind to me for saying other. I saw novices being grievous hurt and beaten by brothers who were filled with the rage of the devil in them. Some took pleasure from this violence in their souls and beat boys often and for no good reason. I was large built for my age and only suffered a few beatings. This is not what troubles my soul but the other wickedness practised by some brothers, the wickedness of the male body that rises in their organs and makes them seek release where-so-ever it might be found. Some went to the settlement to lie with women even though their vows forbade this. Others sought release with boys who were novices. Many boys were sore distressed by this practice being confused and frighted to say no or refuse their master. When first I was given this temptation I gave the service demanded. I was too frighted to say what was in my soul. I knew this was wrong and not a thing we should give in to in our selves or in others. After I confessed to the Prior, Abbot Find Barre being gone travelling on his ministry, the Prior was kind but said he would not act against the master who had done this thing to me. He said it was for each to find his own true path and I must take mine. I did and never gave release to a brother again, suffering a few beatings in my refusal. Soon the others knew I was not to be made to do what was not in me and they stopped asking me. It sore troubled me and it set me on a path that led me away from the Abbey of Find Barre seeking a more austere place where temptation was not to be found.

Many sailing boats began to come to Coracgh to trade. It grew bigger with each passing month it seemed and soon the hovels of the poor spread up the hills and pressed hard on the walls of the Abbey. We were charged with ministering to the bodies and souls of the poor and the travellers. We read the scriptures to them and tended their wounds and fevers.

Many brothers fell ill while tending the people and plagues and fevers took a great harvest on our Abbey. In one year we were kept busy days and nights burying or burning the many dead of the town and the Abbey when a great plague took many score and hundreds of souls.

One sailing master told me of a place he'd stopped and spoke of a few monks who were trying to build a new monastery there.

He said a man called Fionan lived there alone for many months. The island was but a rock surrounded by sea and two hours hard rowing from the shore. The thought that I should go there entered me and would not give me peace ever after.

I have looked into my soul seeking a reason why I was not content with the life at the Abbey of Corcach. My masters taught me much and I studied more than many novices. I saw that perhaps I might be suited to the life of a scribe for it is solitary and still and that suited my nature. After my vows were taken I worked in the scriptorium.

This was pleasing to me and I learned much transcribing old manuscripts on to new parchment. Many of these old documents had been brought from afar. Many from the old holy city of Rome. Many of the Latin words were not known to me and I tasked my master by asking often what words meant. He said I need not need know to transcribe faithfully. I believe now he knew little of the meaning himself and said this to hide his shame.

The one work of the scriptorium I did not care for was the preparing of the parchment. The liming and scraping of the sheepskins was odorous and hard. My hands often were sored and bleeding from the lime and the scraping tools. When the skins were clean and dried and stretched on the frames the work seemed good. Cutting the skins to size and then scribing a new parchment gave me much pleasure and made the task rewarding in the end.

I asked to be given to a new master and the Prior moved me in the end. Brother Luan knew many more ancient words and could read the ancient Greek. He was glad to teach me this and more of the Latin. As my understanding grew I became hungry for the wisdom of the ancients. I would read more than I needed to and tasked Master Luan by being late to devotions. I lost the time in my reading and study.

My thoughts kept going to the island place, the name I later learned was: the Great Skellig. I dreamed of a life of reading, study, work and contemplation of the mysteries I was learning of more each day.

When I had reached my nineteenth or one score years, I told the Abbot I intended to go to the Skellig. He had not heard of this place and thought it might be a tale of the sea like the silkies or the mermaids and sirens of the old tales. But still he wished me well and gave me a beautiful scripture to carry with me and a script introducing me to the Prior or Abbot of the Skellig, if there was one.

I spoke to the boat people and asked to be told if one came that might go to the Skellig.

I had to wait near six months before I found a boat that would take me near. It was sailing to the island of Valencia, which I was told was near enough to my destination. The captain of the vessel told me he knew the Skellig rocks but he'd never stopped there. He said going ashore might be very difficult and he was not prepared to risk his boat. He told me there would be boatmen that might take me at a place called: Allaghee Beg.

The journey started easy and lulled me so my fright was slight but I learned that what I thought was the ocean was only the great inlet of the Coracgh that went on for near all the first day. When we sailed through the narrow place that marked the entrance, we suddenly were rising and falling and plunging in swells that towered above the sails of the boat. Then I was frighted and soon was much afflicted with sickness that caused me to hurl over the side all the day and into the night. I prayed much for relief but none came that night or the next. On the third day the sea was all at once still and calm and the sickness left me. I was put to work at the oars with the others for the sail had failed with no wind to blow it.

The work at rowing was hard but I was glad of the labour to keep my thoughts from the fears that came to me. We put in at a small settlement where the boatmen traded with the people. They brought salt beef and wine in skins and traded for butter and cheese and some fresh milk and fouls in feather. I tried to speak to the people and read the scriptures as the Abbott said was my duty. In truth the people were not much caring for my words and laughed and mocked me for my strange speech and sounds. I knew well then that the life of the mission of conversion was not for me and I was glad I was going to a life away from the taunts and laughter.

When we came to the place of Valencia I went ashore and was told the way to Allaghee Beg. The local people said it was days walk over the hill they pointed to. They also showed me were to look for the islands in the sea called the Skellig. As I rose up the side of the hill I could see the two isles not very afar. We had sailed past them on the journey and the boatman had told me these were the Skellig but I'd thought he was mocking. The steep rocks shaped like a great point seemed far too strange and foreboding for any but the great seabirds to live upon. Now I knew where my destination lay, I was for a time filled with dread and sat upon the heather staring at the pinnacles rising from the sea. A great loneliness came upon me and I longed for the comfort of my home and hearth and the comforts of my mother and brothers and father.

The Skellig Islands from Valencia Island.

I prayed for guidance and a sign that I was on the path the lord had set for me. After, I shed tears and was struck low by doubts, that sign came suddenly when the looming dark of the sky parted and the light of the sun shone in a great stream on the Skellig alone. The isles then lost their fear for me and I saw that the fright of their prospect was the very thing that made them the place for a hermitage and monastery to be. The place where peace might be found, far from the noise and laughter and concerns of the people who strive in the settlements and villages and farms.

When I reached the summit of the hills I could see plain the inlet from the sea that was my destination and the Skellig beyond. I reached the place in the evening time. Too late to seek a boatman. I stood near the water and saw a few black curragh upturned on the field by the shore. I crawled beneath one and made shelter there for the night. I had some hard-bake oatcakes and had gathered a small bag of hedgerow blackberries. This was my supper.

Next morning I was startled and waken by the curragh being lifted off me. The boatman was as frighted as I at first but when he saw my hair and robes he laughed and knew what I was and where I wanted to go. He spoke of other brothers who had been taken to the isle before me and how he made the journey once a month to bring them milk and other victuals. He said there were but four brothers and they laboured hard to build shelter and cut steps up the cliff and gather seabirds and eggs and shellfish. He told how they gathered sea plants to lay on the rock so that they might make earth to grow plants to eat in future times.

Abbott Fin Barre had returned to me the gold coin I had when I came first and he gave it to me to pay for my passage. I had some silver coin left and gave it to the boatman to take me to the isle. The sea was not as still as when I arrived and I worried I might be sick again. I clung so hard to the curragh the man laughed at me. Making the shore was a sore test of my courage, as I had to leap to the rocks with the curragh rising and falling as high as my length. I managed in the end but hurt my hands on the rough rocks when my sandals found no purchase on the weed slipped shore. I was standing looking at the bleed and trying to not drip it on my robe when I was called from above. He said, "Brother have you come to join us?"

I said yes and told him I had a parchment from Abbot Finn Barre. He told his name was Fionan.

The place I landed was a precipitous shelf of rock barely above the waves. There were a few rough steps hewn in the rock that led to were the brother stood above me. I climbed and when I stood before him he took me by the shoulders and kissed me on either cheek. This surprised me but the welcome in the gesture lifted my spirit.

The climb up the steep cliff made me frighted for my life but Brother Fionan said they where working on steps on the south side of the island to make the journey up less danger. When we got near the top, I saw that there were two peaks to the island with a flat place in between. The brothers had been labouring to make fields of earth here and had planted some crop. Oats and cabbages and some other thing I learned later were called turnip. Fionan showed were a deep hole in the rock gathered rain so there was fresh water to drink and cleanse. He also showed me the latrine. This was a big stone overhanging a great fall

into the sea. There was a basket of moss and wood hut
above for a roof. He laughed and told me none had toppled
yet but to make sure I never used it when much exhausted
so sleep might come upon me unexpected. At first I saw no
dwellings and wondered where we might take our sleep.
We came over a little rise and below in a kind of bowl in
the rock there were dwellings built and being builded.
They were domed, as tall as a man and made from flat
rocks piled one upon the other. I'd never seen dwelling of
this kind and marvelled at the intelligence of the
construction. Fionan told me they would teach me how to
build my own dwelling but I could share his till this was
done. Another larger building was being built and two
brothers could be seen labouring at this. "That will be the
oratory," said Fionan. He turned then and pointed across
to the other peak saying, "We are building several smaller
there for retreat and contemplation."

"Hermitage?" I asked.

He answered yes and said those brothers drawn to life here seek hermitage and the dwellings where we stood were not for true contemplation and communion.

The cells on Skellig.

CHAPTER THREE

Skellig Beginning.

The other two Brothers came to be introduced to me. I was surprised to see that Brother Feifhlim and Óengus were older than me by at least twice and Fionan was perhaps ten years older. I called him Abbot but he said he was not Abbot and that they had no Abbot or even Prior. He told me they decided what they would do after the Compline devotion each evening. He said I should speak my thoughts at this time on any matter I wished.

Until a dwelling could be built for me, I would share with Brother Fionan. He said I should spent the day gathering dry moss and what I could to make a bed. He showed me they had cloth for the making and needles and twine for stitching. Brother Feifhlim said he would walk with me and show me where I could walk with safety and where I might find good dry moss and hay.

I was filled with questions but was unable to find my voice. It seemed too much and in truth I was frighted to the very depth of my self. The place was so harsh and unfriendly to life. I could not see how we might make a monastery in this place. The three who came before me all seemed, to my eyes, weak and hungry. They looked like people I've seen who were close to death.

Feifhlim must have sensed my unease and laid a hand on me to stop me and spoke. He said, "Brother do not let fear grip you. We who came first made mistakes and built good dwellings first when we should have put our labour into making earth for food. We came near death from starvation this past winter. We have learned well our lesson and now we have ways to gather sea birds and eggs and fish and shells and we have crops growing."

I laughed and was right amazed that he had seen my thoughts and fears.

I built a bed and stitched it with the needle and twine I always carried in my shoulder bag. The other brothers were glad to see I had these things and all stood before me and had me repair tears and rips in their robes. I decided I did not want to share a cell and so set off to go to the hermits cell on the peak opposite the monastery cells. It was a stiff climb and the cell was very small. Only big enough to lay my bed. As I knelt at the entrance to do my evening devotions I was struck, as if by a blow, by the sight beyond. The small green field the brothers called 'the saddle' leading to the peak with their cells and the oratory clinging to it's edge and the great sea all around. It sang its song of restless movement always so true silence was a rare thing. I saw great flocks of white sea birds coming to the island cliffs to nest for the night. Some small fast flying ones landed near me. They where comic looking like tiny men with painted faces. They lived in holes in the ground and were noisy and confused as they searched for their homes. As darkness came they grew silent.

I remained kneeling and felt a great peace upon me. My spirit soared to the heavens and I knew this feeling was what I had read of in the ancient creek manuscripts. They called it being outside your self. Their word was: ec-static. This I felt and was sure then that the labour and the hardship of living in this Skellig was the only true place for me and was where God ordained I should be to worship his glory.

The three months after I arrived was spent in hard labour building my cell. The rock was hewn from the cliff and Brother Feifhlim had the idea that if I tore the stone from the cliff edge it would make steps as I laboured. Thus a path was made to the boat landing as I made my cell. I soon suffered the pain of soft hands for I had many blisters and cuts. My back grew sore and my arms and legs pained me every night. With time my hand grew hard and my muscle grew used to the toil.

I should have accepted more of the offered guidance in the method of building one stone upon the other in a circle getting smaller as it rose until the final stone sealed the dome. My pride made me refuse help and that pride was rightfully punished. My first cell was near the death of me when it collapsed down on me as I slept my first night in it. My brothers heard my cries and toiled for an hour to get the stones from off me. I was sore bruised but blessed not to be broken or mortal injured.

I did suffer an injury that cost me much work a few weeks later. While cutting stone, a sharp fragment flew and pierced my left eye. Brother Fionan pulled it from my eye with great care but a little must have remained for my eye swelled 'till I could see nothing from it. A poultice was made from sea plants and I wore this over my eye held with cloth. The wound would not be recalled now but for what befell me because of it. I was a stubborn young man and would not be confined to my cell. I determined to work on. I went gathering the sea birds from the cliff, a thing I had been adept at. We oft climbed down the precipitous sea cliffs to gather eggs and pluck the birds from their nests and perches. I used to be fair amazed they showed no fear of me and would sit while I reached for them.

On the third day after my eye was wounded I went gathering in the evening dusking. I had three plump birds in my bag and was intent on three more. I had to cross a gap and misjudged the distance, finding I could not measure well with one eye.

I plunged into the void. I still see clear my thoughts, as I fell. I was sure I'd be dashed on the rocks and waited for the blow with strange stillness in my soul. The passing time seemed to slow so I had many thoughts and saw my life and my parents and my home and sisters and brothers. I tried to think of God or the blessed Jesus but my mind would not rest on the hereafter.

I saw the rocks rush to me and then something happened that I now think was the hand of God. A great breath of wind came and cast me out over the sea so I fell in its waters and not on the rocks. The shock took knowing from me for a little time. When I awoke, I was under the waves and was sitting on the bottom, as if reposed. I tried to rise but the wetting of my robe was too heavy. I knew I must take it off and struggled to do it. Then I rose and came to the air gasping for the breath to sustain my life.

I knew how to swim for I had spent many hours in the lake at our home. I came to the rocks and climbed upon them. The cliff above was mighty and I knew I could not climb up. I had to go back in the sea and swim to the boat landing place. It took a long time and I had to come to the rocks to rest often. It was dark night when I reached the place and climbed out. I could hear the voices of my brothers calling to me above and when I found my breath I shouted to them.

Twice since I came to the isle I was tested and came near death and it caused me to question if God wanted me to have this life.

CHAPTER FOUR

Questions.

I went to the hermitage and searched my soul with questions. I stayed until my eye was healed. The brothers gave me what I asked for and let me lie in the hermit cell undisturbed. I drank only a little water and took no food for many days. I was weak and thin and my thoughts journeyed strange, as I lay in the stillness of the cell.

This was the first test of my faith I faced. I could not escape the torment of an idea that gripped me. That idea was this: I am not meant to be here or anywhere. I am not called or destined to follow any path laid for me by God. I am here because I choose this path, it's not God's choosing.

The scriptures did not offer me guidance, for in truth, I had always struggled to retain in my memory all I had read or been taught. I seemed not to have the facility to learn in that way. The small scripture that I carried with me was near but I did not want to seek answers there. The decision not to seek answers in the holy book was what gave me fearful thoughts I might be losing my faith.

I remembered reading in ancient Greek scrolls ideas that seemed to me heretical when I was transcribing them. My masters had told me not to be concerned with meaning and to think only of the faithful reproduction of the script into Latin.

The ideas described in the ancient arguments spoke of men having the freedom to choose their path and that this was the burden of all thinking beings. Choice. Unlike the beasts who follow the nature of their creation on paths that do not change. Like cattle that are as all cattle have been and always shall be. They do not wonder and question what they must do and be but follow the nature of being cattle that they are born with. They do not have the burden of choice that so troubles men.

I also remembered reading a manuscript that came from the holy city of Rome that spoke of the fall of man, when he was tempted by Eve and chose a path that led him away from the path of God so he was forever cursed with the heavy burden of having to choose between the good path of God and the evil of his own desires and unconfined appetite.

I now saw that this burden of choice was what weighed so heavy on me. It was I who chose to climb on high rocks while my vision was impaired. Pride had led me to foolishness and danger. It was not the will of God or any other force but that within me. Like Adam, I had been tempted and had taken the wrong path. If I had not been raised on a great water, where swimming was taught me by my brothers, then I would have perished in the sea.

This was none of it the work of God but the choices of men. The choosing was mine and living or dying was in the hands, not of God, but of my own. My own hands that dragged me to the rocks and out of the death the sea promised.

The lesson in this came slow to me but the lesson was well learned. I must think more about the steps I took and not believe that my life was in the care of God. My soul and my sprit was his but not my life. I needed to consider more the everyday choices I made if I were to stay alive long enough to serve God in the ways I thought I should.

The questions that came to me as I lay in my cell were, I am sure, created by my state. I had not eaten for days and was weak and fevered. I now know I must have been close to death. The brothers visited me everyday and brought me food and water but in my fevered state I refused their aid. Brother Fionan sat with me and poured broth in my mouth, encouraging me to swallow by pinching my nose. He fed me even when my will refused. To him I should have owed my life. In his view I would surely have perished if he'd accepted my stubborn refusal. This is not so.

I have oft questioned why I withdrew in this way and seemed to be seeking death. I believe I had no such idea. I at no time thought deaths arms encircled me. I had withdrawn into my own self so completely; I seemed to others on deaths steps. I think if I'd been left alone I would have fed when I needed to and stirred myself when needed. Our flesh is vital and can live longer than we fear if our spirit is strong. Brother Fionan came again with broth and I sat up and refused him, saying, "Leave the broth and I shall sup when I am ready. I do not need you to force me."

He accepted and left me in peace and repose then.

I took the broth that night in the dusking. I sat by the cell door and looked at the great sea and sky made one by the darkness so I could not see where sky met sea. The numberless stars of the night drew me upwards in wonder and awe. I had often watched the sky and knew the stars moved in time. This movement I found wondrous and spent long hours trying to see why the heavens moved. Why did day follow night and the sun and the moon sweep the sky in regular movement the same every day but changing with the months and seasons. This wonder was, I saw, the same wonder that perhaps helped man see the work of God for what else could explain these things so huge and unknowable.

I had always been one to question, never accepting things without thought and consideration. I had read of this way of being and knew it was given the name: 'sceptic' by the wise men and ancient Greeks. My tutors at Fin Barres school were sore vexed by my questions and called me Sceptic. But they meant this as insult. Obedience is one of the vows of the monk and one I took but it was one I broke often, if only in my thoughts. My sceptic thoughts were I think what drove me to find solitude and a different life on Skellig.

I gave devotions and prayed as the others of my new brotherhood did but we were not so strict in our devotions to the hours. We respected the need for the hermit's way of giving devotion, so being absent from prayer at vespers or lauds was not considered a great sin. Often we could give devotions alone in our cells or in the hermitage or while labouring.

On the tenth day of my isolation I tried to read my scripture and found I could not make my eyes see. The wound had healed and I could see from my sored eye but somehow it had lost the reading of words. At first I was frighted and worried I might never read again but I found if I covered my wounded eye then the other could find the meaning in the words. All at once I knew why I had fallen from the precipice.

With one eye I could see but I needed two to measure distance. By experiment I discovered I could not place my finger on a spot on the cell wall with one eye closed but could with two. Then when I looked at the script with first one eye and then the other I saw that each eye had changed so each saw a different measure. This loss was, I prayed, a thing that might yet be cured by time but I worried gravely that my sight would be disturbed forever more.

I could not foresee a life on Skellig if I could not climb and gather eggs and birds or read my scripture. My spirit was sore and brought low and I once again lay in the hermit cell and drifted in the thoughts of my mind and time lost meaning.

I decided after a time, I must leave the isle. I rose and went to find my brothers. We assembled in the new oratory that was nearing it's finishing. I told them of my decision and told the reasons. Brother Fionan asked if I would leave the brotherhood and go back to my family and his question made me see I had not considered what I would do. My pause made him say: "You must wait till a path is revealed to you before taking this step."

These were wise words so we agreed I would do what work I could and stay off the precipices until my path was clear.

I took all the wintertime to settle and see what I might do. My eyes got better so I could see well enough to gather and climb but reading was still a one-eye thing.

As the fine weather of Spring came to us we had a new brother arrive to join us. Brother Colm was older than us by a score years and had been much travelled. He had been on pilgrimages to many places and had been a preacher and on missions to convert heathens and barbarians in the lands to the south of the Gaul and Franks.

He spoke to me of the holy city of Rome and the resting place of Saint Peter. I knew then that I must go there to study the great manuscripts that had been brought back there after being rescued and saved in our own monasteries. I was surprised by this, not knowing that the monks of my land had travelled so far and had been so much a part of the saving of the ancient manuscripts when Rome was sacked by barbarians in the past years. I determined I must learn from the wise men of the scriptorium and libraries there.

CHAPTER FIVE

To Rome.

I had to wait near a year before I found passage from Fin Barres monastery at Coracgh across the sea to Normandy. I had been well prepared by my brothers who had gone before. They gave maps and instruction on how to make the journey. They told where I might find sanctuary and sustenance on the long walk to Rome. That journey was long and at times hard and fearful to me. I saw things and places I could not have dreamed. My path took me to a few cities the like of which I could not have foreseen. At one, Rouen, the first I came to. I abided in a monastery there that surpassed the whole of Coracgh in size and numbers. The buildings of stone reached to the heavens and the oratory, called a cathedral, was beyond my words to describe.

The riches of the place were untold and made me wonder what nature of monks these were, for their wealth seemed not to sit well with the vows I had taken. I began to see that my brotherhood was one I had read of called: 'ascetic.'

This had not been a word or a meaning I understood before I saw the way monks lived at Rouen. They feasted and drank ale and wine. The cathedral had gold and silver and jewels and the Abbot was a fat and powerful man like a king or lord. I was made welcome there but I was uneasy and did not tarry long but set out after two days. I began to see that the faith I was raised with and the vows I took were not universal and that many kinds of faith were practiced. All most as many as there were abbeys and settlements. I heard many tongues I could not understand and only was able to speak when I found an abbey. There Latin was spoken. But even then the ways it was sounded was difficult and I began to see that the voices of men are made where they are born and raised.

I also learned of the great debate in the faiths that I had not been aware of at home. Monothelitism is the teaching that Christ has only one will, the divine will, in contrast with the teaching that he has both a divine will and a human will. Monothelitism was what I was taught. I also discovered that in Ireland the devotions of Easter was held to be at a different date to that practiced in many other places.

I will not relate all the tales of my journey for they were many and some are now lost to me as I write this many years later.

When I approached Rome, I was weary and the leather of my footwear was wore through. The site of the great city lifted my spirit and frighted me truly as well. I had never cast my eyes on such a grand and huge settlement. Its buildings were of great antiquity and yet far in advance of anything I'd seen in Ireland. It took near a day to traverse the city and I wandered off in roads not knowing to where they led. I knew I must find the river Tiber and cross it and there I would find the Basilica Sancti Petri. I asked many before I found one who understood my Latin and who's Latin I could know.

When I stood at last before the place that holds the bones of Saint Peter, I was made stupid and my mouth hung open. I had never seen or could never have imagined so mighty a building. When I entered in, I stood before five isles that led to the centre. There the roof stood maybe eighty or one hundred times my height, as if suspended from the sky by Gods own hand. There were more people inside than ever I'd seen before. I estimated there must have been three or four thousand souls gathered for the mass. I asked a fellow brother and he told me the mass was led by the Holy Father himself: Papa Honorius. This Pope is said to be the descendant on earth of Saint Peter, who lay in faults beneath the place he stood to say the mass.

I was moved and confused and found tears in my eyes as I stood with so many others in this holy place. The mass was like none I'd ever seen and was difficult to follow. I was at the back of the multitude and could not hear the voice of Papa Honorius.

After I remained as the people left. I found a father of the church and presented my letters from Fin-Barre. I was astounded to be spoken to in my own Irish. The father had come to serve in Rome ten years before. His Irish was not mine and I struggled to follow so we spoke in Latin. He said the Irish brothers and church were much talked about now, as the holy father was trying to get them to change the date of Easter to the same as Rome and the rest of the lands about. He mentioned a place I had read of, Constantinople, the seat of the Byzantine emperor who rules Rome and who even the Holy Father had to bow to. I was told the Greek language was used much in the empire and asked if I could speak it. I had to say no not speak, only read.

This was a great delight to Father Paul. He asked if I would like some work in the great scriptorium translating certain old scrolls and manuscripts. I was sore troubled when I had to tell of my eyes not being able for good reading anymore. When I told him how this came to be and told of how I could only read with one eye, he grasped my hand and dragged me with haste through the mighty church and through passages at the rear. We came to a small room and he took me in and gave me to the care of an old man surrounded by strange devises and bits of clear glass. I was truly shocked beyond words by what he did. There were many experiments holding glass before each of my eyes and asking me to read script before. Then he worked at bench for a small time then gave me glass held in wire that sat on my face before my eyes. I was cured. I could read with both eyes. I was speechless and unable to give proper thanks. He called the magical instruments: 'vitra-spectacula.'

He tied a string of leather to the sides. This held them on my head so I might work without fear of the spectacula falling from my nose upon which they rested. He said I need only wear them to read.

I was saved and my life took a new path because of these instruments.

I was given lodgings within the buildings of the Basilica Sancti Petri. The food was richer than I was used to and some of it was strange to me. Again I was struck by the difference between how these holy men lived and what I had been raised to see as the role of the monk. Some of the priests and monks and bishops and abbots were very fat and had great riches. Some lived in palaces near the Basilica. I found myself made unsettled by this and I longed for the simplicity of my life on Skellig. I was put to work in one of the many scriptorium, translating ancient Creek manuscripts to Latin. This I liked well and I worked all day, but for devotions, and on into the night.

I must tell the truth and say I was trying to hide from the sights that so upset me and made me question the faith of the men who dwelt in the holy city. Their concerns seemed not to be for living a life as intended for holy men. They seemed concerned with money and power and politicking. This was a word I had not known before I came to Rome.

I enjoyed my work and was reluctant to do anything else. On one day, I did walk in the city. It was good to see the old places but the crowds of people living close one upon the other and the smells and dirt and noise were difficult for me. I came upon an area where the people were very different. Very dark skinned and they dressed unlike their fellow Romans. I saw that I was in the Judah area. I was standing looking at one of their places of worship when two men came out and spoke to me. They spoke in Latin. They asked me what a Christian was doing at this place and they seemed to me worried or frighted. I told them where I was from and what I was doing in Rome and said I was not meaning harm or offense but was curious because I had never met people of their faith. They seemed surprised that none of their faith were in Ireland and said their people wandered far over all the countries.

We talked for a time as we sat on a bench near. We spoke of the manuscripts I worked on and they asked if I had come upon any about their people. I said I had not but had been given a scroll that had marks upon it that looked like the marks above their place of worship. They told me it was their Hebrew language. They said many of their texts had been lost in Rome when the barbarians came and sacked the city in past times.

I remained in Rome for four years. The time past quickly and I learned much. I walked out side the city and explored the ancient sites of the Roman Empire. I found the people to be friendly and welcoming. My robes seemed to give me special status and I was oft fed and given water or wine to sup as I travelled.

After the four years I began to feel a keen desire to return to Skellig. I was sure that the life of cities and big abbeys were not suited to me. I was made sure when the master of the scriptorium changed and a new one came. He began to be a bother to me and the other younger brothers. As I have said, some brothers seemed unable to keep chaste and wanted their earthly desires satisfied. They often turn to younger brothers or boys. I found this not often but enough to pain me and wish to be away back to Skellig.

I had friendship of the Prior of the order from the monastery at Glendalough in the mountains of Wicklow. It was he who I first met in Rome. He was going back to

Ireland too and we decided to travel together. He was a man of some wealth and had two horses and a wheeled cart to carry his chattels. He was taking manuscripts back to be transcribed. I helped him load these in his cart. It was good not have to carry any satchel or bag. We had good food and wine and even beds to sleep upon under the cart. It made the long road easy and we talked much as we walked.

I shall never regret my going to Rome but I was keen to be home to a simpler life that I had sore missed.

The path from the sea on Skellig.

CHAPTER SIX

Skellig again.

My journey back to Skellig took half a year. The brothers there were surprised at my arrival and greeted me warmly. Five more had arrived and so now, with me, there were nine. I was sad to learn that Brother Fionan had died in the past year. He had like me, fallen from the precipice but he fell upon rocks and was killed. His body was swallowed by the sea deeps.

This death made me think and wonder about why Fionan had been taken and I spared. He had been the one who first came to build the monastery on Skellig. As far as I could see he was the fairest and most devoted of the brothers and yet he was taken while still a robust young man. Once again I was taken back to the teaching and readings that said that we, all men, are burdened with free will, the ability to choose our path and that path is not determined by God or any other power. I have heard many people who call themselves Christian say, "It's in Gods hands." Or "It is his will." I can see why people struck by grieving and loss might find comfort in that idea. But I began to think that is a foolish way to think and be and makes grief and loss and death more likely to happen. Anyone who treads the dangerous roads life lays before us without learning of the dangers and trying to avoid them by planning and thought and taking pause when the path ahead is unclear or unseen; is surely being foolish and even stupid.

We all have in us the possibility of learning and reason and imagination so we may light our path with the knowing of those who have gone before on the same path.

I spent the first few months after my return in the hermitage cell. My old cell was occupied and there were none others. I set to build myself a new one. As I sat outside the hermitage looking across the saddle between the two peaks, I was often amazed by how much had been built since I went away. The oratory was finished now and there were three more cells. The saddle between the peaks was green with planting and much labour had been done bringing sea plants up to make new earth for growing.

Once my new cell was finished, I came back to the community and once again entered in to the ways. We now met in the oratory for devotions, prayer and meetings to speak of plans. One thing had changed since I'd been away. A new monastic settlement had been built on the mainland at a place called Ballinskelligs. There was a growing community there and they offered support to us on the isle. They sent supplies on a boat once a month and asked if some of their brothers could come to us on hermitage. Over the next years new brothers would come to us to find peace and silence and seek the gift that hermitage reflection can bring to the soul. I have to admit I did not welcome these visits. I liked it better when we had isolation that was complete. I oft questioned what it was in me that made me seek this isolation and quietude. I was never at ease when in the company of others.

When I had been settled into the ways of Skellig again, the time past unnoticed and months became years. Then an event happened that changed our lives forever more. It was early in the summer; the weather was fine and warm. I was on the north cliff gathering birds eggs. I was suspended on a long twine. We were careful of falling now and always used a twine tied to a stout rock at the top to prevent falling.

I saw a boat with sails approaching. It was large and of a type I'd not seen before. Long with a rising to the front and back that had what seemed to be a carved figures.

There were many on this long boat, I counted twenty men. They were not Irish for many had golden hair. They wore beards and some had metal helmets upon their heads. I am not sure if they saw me but I did not wave to them for they frighted me and I was well to be frighted. The sailed past me but close to the isle. After a time I began to climb back up but stopped when I heard dreadful screaming. There were sounds I'd never want to hear again echoing around the peaks. Then I heard voices above me. A strange tongue I didn't know. When I looked up it was as if I was looking into the face of a demon. One of the golden hairs stood above. He held a great axe and he was covered in fresh dripping blood. He cut the rope with the axe and I fell a little but clung to the rocks. I watched to see if he would climb down but he didn't. He went away. I waited long until I saw their boat again. It was being rowed by many oars towards the shore.

When I climbed back, what I found - I cannot find words to say well. All my brothers were slain. They lay butchered like beasts. Blood flowed like rivers down the steps. Three lay in the oratory cut down while praying. Their heads severed from their bodies. One I found was split from shoulder to groin as if butchered like a pig. I ran to the hermitage and stayed there praying for three days.

The chalice and cross and some cups were taken from the oratory and all the cells had been gone through as if they searched for prizes. When I emerged the rain had washed the blood but still I had to gather the bodies and bury them in a shallow pit I dug in the growing field. I made a cross and said the rights and prayers for my slain brothers.

Many years later I heard these men were called Norse and they were much feared. They came again and again to raid and they came to Coracgh and burned the city and killed many hundreds and made off with gold and silver and cattle and women. They came again to Skellig too but that was many years after and I shall tell of that at the proper time.

CHAPTER SEVEN

Rebuilding.

There was a settlement of brothers who made a monastery on the land called Ballinskelligs. I went there to stay for a time to try to see what I must do. The brothers there had been set upon by the Norse the same day they came to the island. A few were killed but many could run away and hide in the forests. All their ale, *fuisce* (Water of life or early whiskey.) and food and some cattle and pigs and all the gold and silver were taken and many buildings fired. I set to help them build new. I spent a year there toiling and finding peace in my labours. A few new brothers came and we spoke of returning to the Skellig to start anew.

In the springtime we came back and planted crops and brought some foul and two milk cows. It was a mighty travail getting the beasts up the cut steps and steep sides. We had to tie them with ropes and all of our strength was exerted pulling and heaving them up to the field atop the isle.

Now with the wisdom of age and looking back, I see it was folly to take milk cows there. When they had eaten the long years growth there was little else for them but our crop of barley and oats and the tops of the roots we planted. We had not fence to keep them out. After but three months at the end of summer we had to slaughter the cows. We fed well on beef till all were mighty sick of the sight and taste of the flesh. We smoked some but much wasted and was foul and maggoty before we could eat it all but it got us through that winter when we had so little crop. Eating the beef made me see how the sea bird fouls tasted bad. Salty like fish gone off.

Their eggs were good but we could not keep them the year. One brother said if we had a firkin of salt butter we could bury eggs in that and it would keep them good. I knew that butter could be had in the Coracgh and we sent letters to the brothers there asking if they could find a firkin and send it to us.

Six weeks passed before a small wood box arrived packed with golden butter. We were sore tempted to eat it and we did put some in our gruel and oats to taste it well. The eggs we buried there lasted well and we could eat eggs in the winter and they were as near good as fresh.

This was a time of growth and prospering for the monastic brothers of our land. The people opened their hearts to our teachers and many were baptised and welcomed into the church of our lord Jesus. Brothers travelled the lands and crossed the seas to bring the faith to men who had the heathen ways and worshiped many pagan things.

Our monasteries gathered tithes and gold and silver were plentiful. I think the people had begun to be afraid for, death came often as plagues. The north-men raided on the coasts and so the people were sore pressed and welcomed the teachings and the healing and succour of the brothers.

I had become the leader and Prior of our community on the Skellig and I undertook some changes to help us deal with the north-men should they come again. At the top of the paths cut in the rock, we made piles of stones we could cast down on them as they ascended the steps. We had the iron-forger at Ballinskelligs make us swords and pikes that we might fight with. I had seen the slaughter and knew that prayer alone would not protect us from these pagan men who new not mercy or kindness and would slay a man on his knees before them.

It was strange to take up these arms and practise and a few of our brothers refused, saying the Lord God would protect them. I tried to tell them of this folly but they would not hear me.

The practice of arms became less as time past in peace and then Norse, for that is what I now heard them called, did not return.

There were now twelve upon the rock of Skellig and this number was suited to our needs, more we could not sustain and less could not do the labour we needed. That this was the number of our Lords disciples was noted and thought auspicious.

We welcomed brothers from the land who came to reside in our hermitage to do silent reflection or penance. One who came was much troubled and wanted penance severe. He refused food and took only water. He wore thorns upon his legs and lay naked upon the rocks. I spoke to him and tried to understand his pain but he was, I think, lost of sense. He raved and rambled and spoke in tongues so his words were not known to me.

After ten days I found him kneeling in the hermitage weeping and he spoke then plain of the deed he did penance for.

I was sore pressed to understand him for he wept as he spoke but I think I knew him to say this dreadful tale. He was a travelling brother who brought the word to the people in the far places of the land. He was in the north of the land and came upon a dwelling. There seemed no one there and he came in to wait and shelter from the wetting rains. A fire was alight burning turfs. He removed his garments and hung them to dry near the fire. As he sat naked warming he was startled to hear a voice speak to him. It was a sweet voice and he found a naked girl standing behind him. He said things I shall not repeat but he said he was gripped by a great madness of lust for the girl and fell upon her and forced his manhood upon her. He said after he saw that she was but small and young. No more than a child. When he regained his sense he found she was sore distressed and bleeding and hurt on her body. He took great fright and fled and wandered the land mad with grief at his act.

I think the devil got in him. Men's lust for the flesh makes them open to the devils ways. I have seen, even in my short life, acts of badness that test all charity and the teachings of our Lord.

So consumed with regret was this brother, his body failed before our eyes. We tried to comfort him and offer consolations but on one night, he came to us as we were at Compline and screamed like a maddened creature. He said he had sinned many times with acts of the flesh and had even lain with beasts. He then tore is robe off and ran and threw himself off the great cliff to be dashed to death on the rocks below.

This act made me wonder yet again about the meaning of our faith and teachings. I retreated to the hermitage to pray and contemplate and read the books. I remained five days and nights but on the sixth morning my contemplation was disturbed by the dread sight of a long boat with sail I knew, coming to the island. The Norse had returned.

I roused the brothers and we armed ourselves and took up hiding places above the landing place. I counted twenty and six Norse on the boat. Twenty came on the island and began to ascend the step. We waited as long as we dared then rose and cast the rocks and stones down upon them. They were frighted and surprised and six of their number were sore injured and tumbled off the precipice to death. Others had wounds upon them and they went down to their ship. They sailed around the isle looking for another place to come on land but there was but one other place and we were ready there and cast large rocks on them even on their boat. They went away then. We did not see the Norse again for many years.

We got news in that month that they had fell upon the abbey at Ballinskelligs and made off with riches. They slew six brothers and the Abbot, who would not flee from them.

The gravestones of monks on Skellig.

CHAPTER EIGHT

Day on day.

My mind struggles to see the events of this time as each day moves to day on day. Each day the same as the last. Many years of my life are now hard to summon as they were marked by routine and ritual that was always the same. My memory leaps to the events that marked this peace with violence or illness or ill fortune.

Sometimes I can see the times when the weather was cruel and made life hard and food difficult to find or grow. There were many weeks when boats could not land on the isle and we had to get by on our larder of stored foods. The buttered eggs. Dried fish and roots stored in sand. I recall with a smile the time we tried to keep the cabbages in a skin with spirit to keep them. The bag swelled and swelled and when Brother Calum tried to open it, the skin blew and erupted all upon him the most violently odorous green slime. We were prostrate with laughing and could not come near him for many days.

After a passing time of peaceful years our settlement was once again struck down. This time the evil came not with the fierce Norse but an unknown and unseen pestilence that struck us sudden and laid low all but two brothers. The thing hit us in one week in October time. Within four days, brothers were sick with fever, swelling lumps in neck and groin and they coughed blood. Their noses, fingers and toes turned black and seemed to rot away. All died a most horrible death within ten days of being struck. I do not know why me and brother Calum were alone spared but I thought many years later that we were alone in the hermitage when the others were struck down. Perhaps the pestilence came with the boatmen and thence to the brothers and we were spared by our distance from them.

We thought it best to have a great funeral pyre and burn all that had touched the dead. Brother Calum supposed the evil may have been passed from one to another by touch and that was why we were spared. I found that hard to see but we did take care not to touch the dead with bare hands and used sticks to lift their robes and bedding. Now I think he may have been right. We were spared were others in the Ballinskelligs Abby, which was also struck, died after they got the sickness when they touched and handled their dead.

We had to leave the isle for two of us could not do work enough to feed ourselves. Brother Calum went to Fin

Barre's Abby and I set out to walk home to Lough Gur to

meet my family. I was made unsettled by the thinking on meeting my family. I'd had no news of them since I'd left all them years past. I left a boy and now I went back a much-changed man.

Lough Gur in County Limerick

Edan's home at Lough Gur.

The walk back took more days than it needed for I lingered many places to speak to people I met and who gave me hospitality and feeding. They had ideas I would preach the word to them but it was not in me to do that. I was not the kind of brother who feels the burning to convert and preach the word of God and the scriptures.

I sometimes think I was a poor disciple of Fin Barre who's teachings spread far and who sent brothers over the far lands to convert the people and bring them into the fold.

Near a full month after I left the Skellig I came to the Gur. I stood at the portal to the valley and watched for a time. It had changed since my boyish times here. Many more trees had been cleared and the settlement on the hilltop had a large high fence about it. It looked like a fort for fighting off invaders.

My approach had not gone unseen and after a time, three men with fierce dogs running before them came to me. They carried pikes and seemed ready for war until they saw my robes and hair. One shouted the dogs off and I was glad for as they grew near I had been frighted they would attack me.

When the men came close, I knew two to be my brothers. Both the younger of me. I called to them saying: "Brothers it is I, Edan."

They stopped a few paces from me and looked at me with puzzlement but soon, Collom came to me and embrace me saying, "You are but bones Edan. I would not have known you for brother. Come and feed and eat the fat so you get meat on you."

As we climbed the hill they told me the news I feared. My mother and father were both dead. She died of a fever and he was killed in a raid by a tribe from the west.

My brothers and their women took great care to feed me more than I really needed. I was not used to such richness of feeding and had difficulty eating what they set before me. I had beef and lamp and swine and foul more in the time I bided there than in the five years before. I got heavy and my gaunt face filled and health and strength came back to my body. I was shocked by how near to death I must have seemed to them when I came.

The monks' life on Skellig was severe and close to the least needed to live. This only became clear to me when I could see how my family lived. I know they killed and butchered more beasts when I was there than they would in a normal year. I think they feared I would perish if they didn't feed me well.

I soon began to put meat on my bones and was amazed by how it changed how I was in myself. I had been sore depressed and filled with gloom but I found I was now feeling content and pleased with life.

The other big thing about that time at home was being around girls and women. I had forgotten the sound of a woman's voice. My brother's wives and girl children became a fascination to me. I would sit by the hearth and watch them busy at their work and listen to their talk. At first they were whispering and shy around me but soon began to ignore the silent strange monk in the dark corner near the fire. I had not heard my own tongue spoke for so long it took me a month to get the meanings again.

Collom's wife called: Feidelm was a great interest to me. She was very... I am lost in seeking words to describe her for these words suggest feeling that gives me guilt even now. I lusted after my brother's wife and this is sin in many ways. I coveted, I lusted, I wished to be other than I was and wished to renounce my vows and seek out a woman like her. If such another was alive and this I doubt.

She was small in height but seemed not somehow. She had breasts that were very large and full and she showed them often when feeding her infant. I was awed and drawn to watch her and was filled with confusion and afire with unfamiliar feelings in sprit and body. My member was tumescent and gave me much discomfort when I was near her. Her hair was fire red and her skin pale and dotted with little brown spots across her nose and cheeks and arms. Her eyes seemed very round and big and were the colour of new spring leaves, bright green. Her lips were plump and seemed too big. Her body seemed abundant in all that is woman. Her beauty was very unusual but it was beauty of the most powerful kind.

All men who met her seemed struck-through by her so they grew silent and watched her and looked at Collom with fear lest he see their coveting. Collom had grown much bigger than I and was a mighty powerful fighting chieftain of Gur so they feared him.

One day he frighted me by banging me on the back as I stood watching Feidelm playing a game with the children before the dwelling. He laughed and said, "She pulls eyes to her and is impossible not to love, brother Edan. Don't think I don't see how you watch and are trouble by the great hard lust she brings to your loins. You are a man Edan. You may be the church's man but still you are a man and no man can look at my Feidelm without lust springing in him. Don't take fright brother. I know she's faithful to me and will lie with no other while I live. I'm not angered by your watching."

This knowing that Collom knew how I looked upon Feidelm was not to be born. I knew then I must leave my family and go back. I headed for the Abby of Fin-Barre and thought I might rest there before going back to Skellig to try to rebuild our little Abby there.

CHAPTER NINE

Skellig Once More.

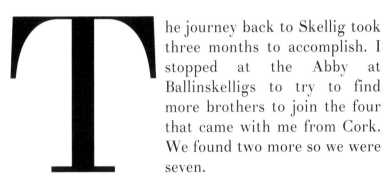

The journey back to Skellig took three months to accomplish. I stopped at the Abby at Ballinskelligs to try to find more brothers to join the four that came with me from Cork. We found two more so we were seven.

We set to planting the seeds that the kindness of the Abbots at Ballinskelligs and Cork had given us. We had some preserved beefs and a firkin of well salted butter. Four firkins of a brew made at Ballinskelligs came too.

Our labours lasted all the month of May then we rested and opened the Ale. For us this was a new thing. It tasted bitter and sweet at the same time and we supped two firkins that day. For the first time in my life I had the drunkenness upon me. I had seen people in this drunkenness but never expected it for myself. I knew that whiskey might do this but had not known that the ale would. We had a fine day and night of much laughter and fooling but next morn all groaned and complained of feeling pained in the head and sick of the body. I spent an hour throwing up great sick at the latrine hole. We knew then that this new ale was near as fiendish as whiskey and we drank it with care for refreshment only from then.

Cut Turf (Bog peat.)

Curragh carrying turf.

I know that day we suffered mightily for we had to carry turfs for our fires up from the boat that came to us from the turf cutters of Ballinskelligs Abby. The turfs are the only thing we have to make our fires for cooking. There being no wood but for some that the sea casts upon the shores we can reach. We all did mighty penance that day. I stopped three times for throwing sickness as I carried the baskets of turfs up the many steps.

The boatmen who came to the island were a brave and fearless breed. They builded their boats themselves from wood and skins of beasts and tar. The tar was a mystery to me and I came to hate it. I had watched a man mending and making boats, they are called 'curragh' in our native words. The tar set in a cauldron, was bubbling over a fire, black and odorous and sticky. I made the mistake of touching a bit the man had put to the boat and my fingers stuck fast on it. I could not pull my hand free and when I did the black stuck to my skin and water would not shift it off. He said if I waited for it to grow hard I could pluck it from me. I noted his hands and cloth were much scarred with the black so no flesh was seen. He even had it in his hair and beard. I took care from that day never to touch the tar on boats.

For the year after I came back from my home, I was troubled by dreams and impure thoughts about Feidelm, my brother's wife. For the first time since I became a monk I had doubts about the life. I also in my fevered state, found release from the torment of my loins with my hand. This was something I'd seen others do and in my postulate years had seen older brothers demand of postulates. I considered this a sin but the rage in me was calmed by the action, so I thought it the lesser evil. Less than coveting my brother's wife or leaving the church and seeking a woman to share a life with.

Those men who cannot live the life of seclusion and celibacy often asked me how I could live this life. It is a question I've puzzled over all my years. I will here try to answer. This answer holds for me alone. I cannot speak for all who take the vows and join the brotherhood or the holy church.

Being alone, alone in body and alone in my thoughts has always been a comfort to me. Even as a child I would seek places to be alone. There to sit and gaze at God's creation in wonderment and adoration. Yes adoration. I was filled with joy at the sights and sounds and smells and tastes of the creation all about me. The singing of birds could stop me walking to stand and listen, moved sometimes to tears by the sweetness of their song. I would rise early to sit outside as light came to the world once more and the singing of morning was loud and busy in greeting the sun. I always noticed when the birds would fall silent in the winter months or when darkness was upon the land. Even then the night creatures would sing and make music in the night. I never feared the dark of night. It held no terror for me, as it does for some.

When I read the Holy Scriptures first, I was seeking answers to these wonders of the world. I found some answer there but not enough to satisfy my hunger for knowing. Later my studies of the ancient scripts of Rome and the Greek wise men that came before Rome, gave more answer. Some of these answers were writ before the coming of the saviour Christ. They seemed to me to be true and in many ways a better salve for my burning curiosity than the Holy Scriptures.

At first this gave me doubts and that doubt was what drove me to seek the silent contemplations and isolation of Skellig. There I could be still and think long about the meaning of what I had learned and what I saw. This more than any other reason, was what made the life of the monk so strong for me. I feel as if with these word's, I am being unfaithful to my order and faith. Saying it was not a need to do God's work or spread the word of the scriptures among the heathen but the selfish need to be alone.

I went to Skellig to seek the comfort of my own thoughts and visions - that this kept me in the brotherhood seems almost a sin. I wanted that isolation and peace more powerfully than I wanted the pleasure of the flesh or the company of a woman and children. That is the truth I see now many years later but then, I saw little but the demands of each day.

We quickly fell to mending the cells and then settled in the daily routine that made each day the same as the last. A boatman asked me how I could stand the day upon day prayers and each day the same as last and all the same? Did I not long for excitements and adventures or travel?

My answer was: "How is our life different from yours? Every day you must toil to feed you and your family and each day holds the same toil and will for the future. We have the comfort of prayer and the thinking on Gods word and work. I have travelled far on Gods work. All the way to the holy city of Rome. I have seen many wonders. But now I am happy here, trying to understand and see how to be closer to God."

In truth I fear he did not understand many of my words for my tongue is not good in the native words. I think in Latin now. Is that not strange? The words of my people and my childhood have left me in my mind so the holy words of the scriptures have taken their place. I must now pause and change words in my mind before I speak to such as the boatmen. We brothers do not talk much but when we do, it is in Latin. All our prayers and incantations are in the Latin and when we met others, even from distant lands, we would talk if we know the Latin. When I went to Rome, all the church people and those at places of pilgrims, spoke in Latin. Brother Ceana, who lives at Skellig, is from the land to the north called Ecosse. I did not know his tongue and he knew not the Irish but we spoke the Latin to each other.

The words in Latin that I consumed so eagerly as a postulate and later in Rome, are the one thing I missed on

Skellig. We had few scripts and no scriptorium or library. I sometimes thought I should go to Cork to the monastery of Fin-Barre, where I could spend each day in the scriptorium reading and transcribing the manuscripts. I thought I should do this soon. Perhaps when I reached my middle years. I was thirty-six years, I think. I'm not sure. My life would be more than half spent then and I wanted my last years to be in the comfort of the scriptorium.

One more attack by the Norse came to Skellig in my final year there. We had not trained for it and we fought them with rocks and such for a little time but they soon overcame us. I shouted for my brothers to flee and to jump in the sea and hide in the sea caves. Most did but Brother Ceana was fierce and he stood at the top of the steps with a sword and fought them. I know he killed one for I saw the blow but he was soon slain. We found his body much hacked and dreadful to see, after. We decided to go ashore to Ballinskelligs but first we spent many months carving a cross and markers for the monument to those brothers who died on Skellig.

I was sad to leave but this time I was sure I would not return.

an Corcach Mó again.

My return to the place I began seemed to make sense, as my life approached it's end. The monastic settlement at Cork had grown and prospered and it was now a community of over four score brothers. It's founder *Fionnbhar* was now gone but his memory remained strong for all who knew the fair one. He seemed to us who knew him, a saintly soul and a great teacher.

I was surprised to be asked by the Abbot to take the role of Sacrist - the Sacrist is responsible for the safekeeping of books, vestments and vessels, and for the care of the monastery's buildings. The surprise came because I was not really aware of my own advancing years. This seems silly now but my isolation meant I did not see the years passing and leaving their mark on me. When I came first the Sacrist seemed to my young eyes to be a venerable old man. I now see he would have been little older than he who takes the role now.

In my work I had many dealings with the people of the town, which had grown large and prospered. A wall had been built about it to try to keep raiders at bay. There were gates that could be closed to keep unwanted out. Since the town was an island surrounded by waters and marsh it seemed a safe and secure place. In my dealings I tried to avoid going down from the Abby into the town. It remained a place too full of people and rank disturbance for my suiting.

I soon settled in my work and must admit I appointed a younger monk as my aid and left much of the work of daily cares to him. I was to be found most in the Scriptorium. I lost all my cares when consumed in reading the words of the ancients and teaching the postulates the Latin and the transcription arts.

When I had been Sacrist for four years I was pleased and surprised to be greeted by a new postulate as revered Uncle Edan. He was the son of my brother and Feidelm. He had his mother's bright eyes and fire red hair and I was once again reminded of the effect she'd had on me. As he spoke I saw great sadness and when I asked why he told me his mother Feidelm had died in the birthing of his little brother. This six months before. This was the reason he was sent to the Abbey and into my care. He said his father could not work well and was often gone for months fighting and raiding and raging in the country. The boy was named for me and was Edan. The other brothers soon named him *Beag*-Edan, (Small-Edan.) This was a little odd. The boy was bigger than me. Like his father in body but with his mother's face.

The rest of my time at the Abby fell into a routine that was comfortable and easy. I lost my awareness of time passing, as I got lost in my studies and readings. Then the time came when the Abbot asked me to write down my story. This story. I thought that was strange but he said those of us who have lived a long life in the service of the church should record our lives for those that follow. And so I set to writing this my testament.

Brother Edan, Corcach. The year of Our Lord 676.

⌘⌘⌘⌘

The story of how men came to build a monastery in so inhospitable and isolated a place as the Skellig islands is a great mystery. Certain men seem to have a need to escape the life they are born into. To escape the natural world and all its harsh and often violent reality. They create new worlds in their imagination and in their religious faith. Often these mystical explanations for life demand isolation and contemplation. It can be no coincidence that so many of the worlds religions include meditation and inward reflection as part of their practise. The seeking of answers within the individual human psyche. Wherever men have chosen that path they also choose isolation and usually in high places. Mountains and peaks harbour and nourish such seeking.

The history of Skellig is largely unknown. Very few references to it exist in the written record. This lack of factual history is at the heart of the mystery that surrounds the islands.

The remarkable preservation of the site adds to the power of the place experienced by those who visit now. We are filled with wonder and questions as to how this was built.

That mystical power is shared by many of the world's great historical sites. Easter Island with it's standing Moai figures.

The lost cities of South America with their pre-Egyptian pyramids.

The pyramids of Egypt themselves are well recorded and have less mystery because of that. But the feat of their building still has the power too astound. Stonehenge in England and the great circles of standing stones, the henges, that men built with ingenuity and astonishing *feats of co-operative effort still amaze us but what makes the monastic settlement of Skellig Michael so utterly amazing, is the fact that it was built not by vast armies of organised men but a few. A few dedicated men labouring for many years driven, by their need for isolation and their faith in their chosen God.*

The End.

David Rory O'Neill.

Newport, Tipperary, Ireland. 2014.

A little of the known history: *(Various sources.)*

Legend ascribes the founding of the monastery to St. Fionan, who lived in the sixth century. The earliest documentary reference to the monastery is an entry in The Martyrology of Tallaght, written near the end of the eighth century by Máel-ruain (d. 792) in his monastery near present-day Dublin. It commemorates the death of a monk of Skellig called Suibni.

To be acknowledged in this manner in the festology of one of the most celebrated monasteries of Ireland, located at the opposite side of the country, Skellig Michael must have been a well-established and widely known monastic settlement. The monastery there may well have been founded as early as the sixth or seventh century, but in the absence of documentation more precise dating is not possible.

The monastery is referred to simply as Skellig in the eighth- and ninth-century entries in monastic festologies and annals (The Martyrology of Tallaght, the Annals of Ulster, and the Annals of Inisfallen).

Sometime after the tenth century the monastery became known as Skellig Michael. It is likely that in the late tenth or early eleventh century the monastery was dedicated to St. Michael. This is suggested by two references to the monastery in the Annals of the Kingdom of Ireland by the Four Masters. The first reads "Age of Christ, 950. Blathmhac of Sgeillic died"; the second, which reads: "The Age of Christ, 1044. Aedh of Sgelic-Mhichil," is the first reliable mention of the name Michael in the annals. On this basis we assume that the dedication to Michael took place between 950 and 1044. It was customary in a monastery to build a new church to celebrate a dedication, and the oldest part of the church now known as St. Michael's fits architecturally into this time period. With its mortared straight walls and large stones, the church is unlike the dry-stone corbeled oratories and beehive cells built earlier at the monastery.

The church of St. Michael was mentioned in The History and Topography of Ireland, by Giraldus Cambrensis, who was in Ireland with the Normans in the late twelfth century (1183 and 1185). His account of the miraculous supply of

communal wine for daily mass in St. Michael's church implies that the
monastery of Skellig Michael was in constant occupancy at that time.

In the thirteenth century, living conditions on the Atlantic islands of Ireland
degenerated to such a degree that year-round occupancy of the island
probably became impossible. A general climatic deterioration, linked to a
southern shift of the circumpolar vortex, began around 1200, and as a result
the polar ice cap expanded. Colder weather and the increasing frequency and
severity of sea storms appear to have forced the monks to withdraw to a site on
the mainland on Ballinskelligs Bay, near Waterville, County Kerry.

Historical as well as climatic reasons explain why in later centuries the
monastery of Skellig Michael never again came into full-time use. Many Irish
monks, imitating the withdrawal of St. Anthony into the desert, sought a
desert in the sea and founded monasteries on hundreds of islands—the
Orkneys, the Shetlands, the Faeroes—eventually reaching from the coast of
Great Britain as far as Iceland.

THE SKELLIG EXPERIENCE VISITOR CENTRE:

Here you can experience many aspects of those offshore Skellig islands while remaining on the dry land, in a custom built, stone clad, grass roofed, prize winning building located right on the waterfront beside the Valentia Island bridge at Valentia, County Kerry!

Here, through re-creations and models you can study the works and lives of the Skellig monks of the early Christian period, their activities, their endurance and their dedication in gaining a foothold on a tiny, inhospitable, offshore island and creating a community there that survived for some 600 years. In The Skellig Experience's 80-seat auditorium, through a 14-minute film presentation you can follow the footsteps of those Skellig monks, and wonder at the legacy of architecture that they left behind.

The Skellig Experience Centre also offers – again through artefacts and realistic re-creations – an experience of Skellig lighthouse – its history – its light keepers and its service to mariners since the 1820's.

In The Skellig Experience Centre the underwater life of Skellig is presented through a gallery of the still photographs of visiting international Skellig divers and through a colourful video exclusively from Skellig waters. The Skellig Experience Centre also includes a restaurant and craft shop.

The Skellig Experience Visitor Centre, Valentia Island, Co. Kerry, Ireland.

Email skelligexperience@live.com

Phone: +353 (0)66 9476306

62446268R00055

Made in the USA
Middletown, DE
22 January 2018